PUFFIN BOOKS

Mummy Fairy and Me

Mermaid Magic

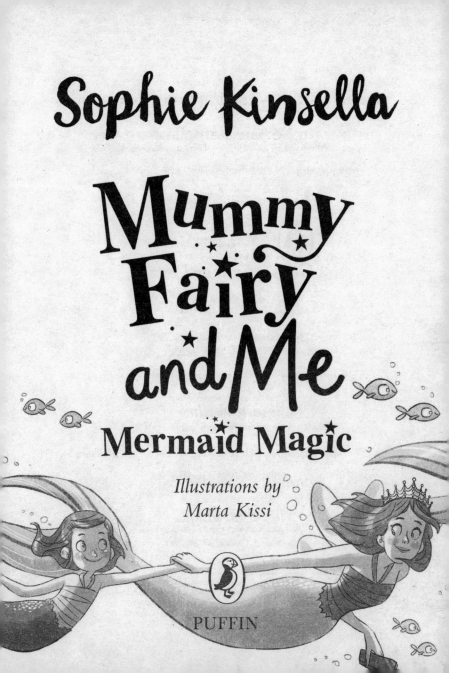

Sophie Kinsella

Mummy Fairy and Me

Mermaid Magic

Illustrations by
Marta Kissi

PUFFIN

PUFFIN BOOKS

UK | USA | Canada | Ireland | Australia
India | New Zealand | South Africa

Puffin Books is part of the Penguin Random House group of companies
whose addresses can be found at global.penguinrandomhouse.com.

www.penguin.co.uk   www.puffin.co.uk   www.ladybird.co.uk

Penguin
Random House
UK

First published 2020
001

Text copyright © Sophie Kinsella, 2020
Illustrations copyright © Marta Kissi, 2020

The moral right of the author and illustrator has been asserted

Set in Bembo Infant MT Std
Text design by Mandy Norman
Printed in Great Britain by Clays Ltd, Elcograf S.p.A.

A CIP catalogue record for this book is available from the British Library

ISBN: 978–0–241–38031–4

All correspondence to:
Puffin Books
Penguin Random House Children's
80 Strand, London WC2R 0RL

For Max and Sophia

CONTENTS

Meet Mummy Fairy and me

Hello. I'm called Ella Brook and I live in a town called Cherrywood with my mummy, my daddy and my baby brother, Ollie.

My mummy looks normal, just like any other mummy . . . but she's not. Because she can turn into a fairy. All she has to do is stamp her feet three times, clap her hands, wiggle her bottom and say, 'Marshmallow' . . . and **POOF!** she's Mummy Fairy. Then if she says, 'Toffee apple,' she's just Mummy again.

My Aunty Jo and Granny are fairies too, because all the girls in my family turn into fairies when they grow up. They can all fly and turn invisible and do real magic. Mummy and Aunty Jo also have a really cool wand called a Computawand V5. It has magic powers, a computer screen, Fairy Apps, Fairy Mail and Fairy Games!

The other problem is that Mummy is still not very good at doing magic spells, even though she works really hard at her lessons on FairyTube with her Fairy Tutor, Fairy Fenella. But one day she's going to get everything right.

When I'm grown up, I'll be a fairy like her too! Mummy calls me her Fairy-in-Waiting. I'll have big sparkly wings and my own beautiful shiny crown, and I'll be able to do magic just like Mummy.

Being a Fairy-in-Waiting is a big secret. I'm not allowed to tell anyone, not even my best friends, Tom and Lenka. And I definitely can't tell my Not-Best Friend, Zoe. She is the meanest girl ever and she lives next door. Sometimes I think she might find out about Mummy being a fairy. But she hasn't yet.

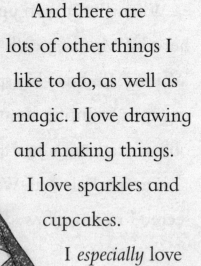

And there are lots of other things I like to do, as well as magic. I love drawing and making things. I love sparkles and cupcakes.

I *especially* love

unicorns and mermaids. Sometimes I wish Mummy could do a magic spell and turn me into a mermaid. If I was a grown-up fairy, that's what I would do. But she always says, 'We'll see, Ella.'

MERMAIDERIDOO!
The Great Whale Rescue

One day we went to the seaside. There was a cafe by the beach and we bought some cakes for a snack.

'What a lovely baby!' said the cafe lady. 'May I hold him?' She took Ollie and he smiled at her. 'Aren't you lovely!' she said to him. 'What's your name?'

'Weezi-weezi-weezi!' he said,

and splatted his cake in her face. She was
covered in creamy icing.

'Ollie!' said Daddy, and he grabbed
Ollie back. 'I'm so sorry!'

'Don't worry!' said the lady, wiping
icing out of her eyes. 'He didn't know
what he was doing, bless him.'

Grown-ups always think Ollie doesn't
know what he's doing. I think he knows
exactly what he's doing.

★

We left the cafe before Ollie could splat
anything else, and went down to the beach.

Daddy carried Ollie on his shoulders and I skipped along on the pebbles.

Daddy showed us how to skim stones on the water. We made sandcastles and Ollie tried to eat the sand. Then Mummy said she wanted to stretch her legs and

have a proper long walk. Ollie is not very good at proper long walks, because he always sits down and cries. So Daddy said he would look after Ollie while Mummy and I explored.

'Make sure you find some buried treasure!' he said.

'We will!' said Mummy. 'Ready, Captain Ella?'

We walked along the beach to a little cliff with lots of rocks at the bottom. We couldn't see past the rocks, so we guessed what we would find on the other side.

I guessed an octopus in a rock pool. Mummy guessed a pirate ship.

We climbed round the rocks – then stopped in astonishment. There was a whale on the beach. An actual real-life whale! It was enormous and it had shiny grey skin.

I was really excited, but Mummy wasn't. She blew out hard and said, 'I didn't guess *that*.' Then she said, 'Whales aren't supposed to be on the beach, Ella. They belong in the water. That whale is in trouble. It's got stuck.'

There were lots of people standing around the whale. Some of them were sloshing water on it. Some of them were on their phones. Everyone looked worried.

When we got closer, Mummy asked a

man if we could help.

The man told us, 'We need to get this whale out to sea.' He explained that once the tide came in they would float the whale back into the water. They hoped it would find its way home.

The whale looked very sad. It was thrashing its tail backwards and forwards as if it was trying to get unstuck from the beach. I wished I could speak whale language and tell it that we were going to help it. Then I had an idea.

'Mummy!' I said. 'Can you use a magic spell and speak to the whale? You could explain that we're going to help it.'

'Yes!' said Mummy. 'That's a very good idea, Ella.'

Mummy went behind a big rock where no one could see her. She stamped her feet three times, clapped her hands, wiggled her bottom and said, 'Marshmallow' . . . and **POOF!** she was a fairy. She pointed at herself, pressed a code on her Computawand – *bleep-bleep-bloop* – and said, 'Inviseridoo!' Then no one could see her – except me, because I'm a Fairy-in-Waiting.

Then Mummy Fairy pressed another code – **bleep-bleep-bloop** – and said, 'Speakeridoo! Whaleridoo! Come on, Ella. Now I can talk to the whale.'

Mummy Fairy carefully made her way through all the people to the whale's head and whispered to it. After a moment the whale stopped thrashing its tail. It seemed to be listening quietly. It even made some whale sounds back. I felt very proud of Mummy Fairy.

A few minutes later, Mummy Fairy came back to me and said, 'The whale is very young. He got lost and needs to find his way back to his mother.'

I felt very sorry for the whale. I know how scary it is to lose your mummy, because I once lost Mummy in a big shop. Since then I always hold her hand really tightly. But whales don't have hands.

'Do you know where his mother is?' I asked Mummy Fairy.

'No. But I know who might be able to help,' she said.

'Who?'

Mummy Fairy bit her lip and said,
'I really ought to take you back to
Daddy . . .'

At once I knew she was going to do
something exciting. 'Mummy Fairy,' I said
quickly, 'please take me too. How will I
learn to be a good fairy if I don't come
with you and help?'

Mummy Fairy laughed. 'Ella, you
always have a good answer. All right,
Fairy-in-Waiting – you can come. We're
going to fly, so I'll need to make you

invisible, and you'll need to hold my hand

tight.'

'I will!' I said. 'I promise!'

I took Mummy Fairy's hand and

squeezed as tightly as I could. She pressed

two codes on her Computawand – *__bleep-
bleep-bloop, bleep-bleep-bloop__* – and
said, 'Inviseridoo! Flyeridoo!'

The next moment we were both
invisible and flying over the sea.

The air was cold and salty. I could see little white waves far below us – and some rocks right in the middle of the sea. We started flying down towards them. I saw a glimmer of silver. It was moving, and I wondered if we were going to meet some seals.

As we got closer my mouth dropped open. Having a fairy for a mummy means lots of surprises. But this was the biggest surprise *ever*.

Sitting on the rocks were two mermaids.

They had long silver fish tails and long dark hair – and they didn't look happy to see us.

'Stay very quiet, Ella,' said Mummy Fairy as we landed gently on the rocks. 'Mermaids are very scared of humans – and fairies too, even though we are friends.'

I had never seen real mermaids before. We sat on the rocks and Mummy Fairy talked in a low voice in a language I couldn't understand. Gradually the mermaids started to look less worried. They all nodded at each other.

'I've asked the mermaids to guide the whale back to his mother,' said Mummy

Fairy. 'I'll make them invisible too, so they will be quite safe.'

One of the mermaids smiled at me and I waved at her. Her eyes were sea-green and there was seaweed woven through her hair. I thought she was beautiful.

'Hello,' I said, even though I didn't know if she could understand me.

She gave me a little pink stone carved with patterns, and I said, 'Thank you!' I put it safely in my pocket.

Then Mummy Fairy stood up. 'We must get back to the whale,' she said. 'We could fly ... or shall we swim?' Her eyes twinkled.

I gasped. 'Can we be mermaids too?' I said, and Mummy Fairy laughed.

'Not real mermaids. But we can have mermaid tails for a little bit. Although it's even *more* important that you stay with me, Ella,' she added. 'You don't want to get lost like the whale.'

She pressed a code on her Computawand – ***bleep–bleep–bloop*** –

pointed it at the mermaids and said, 'Inviseridoo!' Then she pressed another code, pointed it at us and said, 'Mermaideridoo!'

At once I had the strangest feeling. My legs seemed to be growing together. They felt cool and strong and slippery. I looked down and couldn't believe it – I had a mermaid tail!

We all slipped into the water. It didn't feel cold – it felt soft. It didn't sting my eyes like normal, and when I went underwater I realized I could breathe,

even though I didn't have a snorkel!
Mummy Fairy sometimes gets her spells
wrong – but today she had got all her
magic right! Just when we needed it most.

'Ready?' said Mummy Fairy, and she
grabbed my hand tight. Then –

whoosh!

We were zooming through the water. It felt like flying, not swimming.

As we went I saw blue and yellow fish

and a turtle and an octopus. I wished we could be mermaids forever, but before long we were back at the beach. We could see Daddy standing on the sand with all the people, holding Ollie in his arms.

Mummy Fairy swam with me to the shallow water. She did another spell so everyone could see me again and said, 'Go and find Daddy, Ella. Tell him what's happened. I will stay with the whale and the mermaids.'

Just then a man on the beach saw me and his eyes went very wide. 'Little girl!'

he shouted. 'What are you doing? Get out at once! No one is allowed in the water! You might upset the whale!'

Everyone was staring at me, but I didn't know what to do. I couldn't get out because I didn't have any legs, only a mermaid tail.

'Mummy Fairy!' I said. 'I haven't got any legs!'

'Oh,' she said. 'Oops. Let's change you back.' She pressed a code on her Computawand, then said, **'Normeridoo!'**

At once I felt my feet again and started paddling to shore. I missed my mermaid tail, but at least I still had my pink stone from the friendly mermaid.

'Little girl!' said the man again. 'Are you by yourself?'

'She's with me!' Daddy hurried forward. 'Ella, sweetheart, let's get you dry.'

I came out of the sea and Daddy wrapped me in a towel. 'What's your mother doing?' he asked in a low voice.

'Saving the whale,' I whispered back. 'With the mermaids.'

'Ah,' said Daddy. 'I imagined it was something like that.'

★

While everyone was waiting for the tide to come in, Daddy looked around the beach. It was covered in litter. There were cans and old crisp packets and even a broken tent. 'We can't save the whale, Ella,' he said. 'But we can still be useful.'

He stood on a high rock, with Ollie in his arms. He said, 'Attention, everybody! There are lots of special experts helping the whale. But the rest of us can be useful in another way. We can clear this beach so that it is beautiful and clean again. If you want to help, then cheer.'

All the people cheered really loudly! I felt so proud of Daddy. He isn't magic like Mummy, but he is amazing in different ways.

We all started collecting litter. Even Ollie helped. We gathered it into bags and put them at the top of the beach to be sorted out.

After a while the sea started to come up the beach. The waves were getting closer and closer.

'Look!' said Daddy. 'The tide is coming in. It's time for the whale to float back out to sea.'

We went up the steps on to the cliff, so
we would be safe. After a long time the
water was high enough and the
whale slowly began to move
through the water. I could
see Mummy Fairy
and the mermaids

swimming at his side, although no one else could.

Everyone started cheering. 'The whale is saved!' cried a lady with curly hair. 'It's a miracle!'

I knew it wasn't a miracle – it was Mummy Fairy and the mermaids. But I couldn't say that. I just looked at Daddy and we smiled at each other.

When the whale had swum right out to sea, the man in charge of the rescue made a speech. He thanked everyone for their help and said he hoped the whale would find his way home. Then he said, 'And a special thank you to Mr Brook for organizing the litter pick. The beach has never looked so clean!'

As everyone was clapping Mummy crept up to join us. She wasn't a fairy any more. Her hair was wet but she looked very pleased. 'The whale has found his mother,' she said quietly, and I was so happy I gave her a hug.

Then the lady with curly hair said to me, 'Your father is a star. He has made the world a better place.'

I wanted the lady to know that Mummy was a star too, and that she had saved the whale. But I knew I couldn't tell her. So I just smiled and nodded, and said, 'I know.'

★

On the way home I drew some pictures in my book. I drew the whale. I drew the mermaids. I drew Daddy standing on the rock and all the people cheering.

I thought how proud I was of both my mummy and my daddy. I thought about how they had made the world a better place. And I hoped that one day I would make the world a better place too.

VOLCANERIDOO!
Who says science and magic don't mix?

One day after school I was doing my science project at home. Mummy was helping me colour in my poster about volcanoes, but she kept going outside the lines.

'Mummy,' I said, 'Miss Amy likes us to stay *inside* the lines.'

'Sorry, Ella,' said Mummy. Then she

looked at her watch. 'Colouring takes a long time, doesn't it? How about we speed this up?'

I knew she meant she was going to do a magic spell.

'I don't mind doing the colouring,' I said quickly, because sometimes when Mummy tries to speed things up with magic, it doesn't exactly work out. But Mummy didn't listen. She stamped her feet three times, clapped her hands, wiggled her bottom and said, 'Marshmallow!' and **POOF!** she was a fairy.

She got her phone out of her bag, and
I watched as it came alive and turned
into a Computawand. She pressed a code
– **bleep–bleep–bloop** – then pointed
it at the pens on the table and said,
'Colouridoo!'

Straight away the pens flew up from
the table and started colouring my poster
all by themselves! They coloured very fast
and very neatly. I stared at them with
wide eyes, wishing I could colour like that.

'There!' said Mummy Fairy, looking
pleased. 'It just shows –'

45

Then she stopped. She was looking over my shoulder and her face was kind of frozen. I turned round and gasped.

Behind us, all the other pens from my pencil case had flown up and started colouring too. They were colouring in the kitchen cupboards, the ceiling, the lampshade . . . everything!

A blue pen was colouring in the bananas in the fruit bowl. A red pen was colouring in Ollie's face while he laughed and said, 'Weezi-weezi-weezi!'

Quickly Mummy Fairy pressed a different code – **bleep-bleep-bloop** – and shouted, 'Stoperidoo!' At once the pens all fell down, just as Daddy came into the kitchen with Aunty Jo.

Daddy and Aunty Jo looked at all the colourful kitchen cupboards.

'Interesting,' said Daddy. 'Have you been redecorating?'

'No,' said Mummy Fairy, going a bit red. 'I was colouring in Ella's project. The pens got a bit carried away.'

'Tragic,' said Aunty Jo. '*And* the supper's burning.'

'It's not burning!' said Mummy Fairy, looking cross as she rushed over to the oven. 'It's just . . . crispy.'

'If you say so,' said Aunty Jo. 'Shall I give you a hand?'

While Daddy and Mummy Fairy got the supper ready, I laid the table and Aunty Jo turned into a fairy. She cleared up all the colouring with a magic spell, and then made Ollie laugh with magic rainbow bubbles.

Then both she and Mummy Fairy went back to normal and we sat down to eat.

During supper I told Aunty Jo about my volcano science project. My class were all going to a science fair. We would show our model volcanoes and there would be a winner. For my project I had done a poster and a cardboard volcano. I had made lava out of red wool.

'Mummy's going to come to the science fair too!' I told Aunty Jo. 'She's coming on the school coach!'

'Maybe,' said Mummy, sounding a bit

worried. 'But I might have to work that day, Ella.'

Aunty Jo was looking at a leaflet about the fair. 'That's my old friend from Fairy School!' she said, pointing to a picture of a scientist. 'She's called Mai. She was very clever at school. Tell you what, I'll take Ella to the science fair,' she said to Mummy. 'It'll be fun. What do you think, Ella?'

'Cool!' I said.

'But no magic at the science fair,' said Mummy to Aunty Jo.

'I know!' said Aunty Jo, rolling her eyes. 'Of course!'

Mummy and Daddy looked at each other. Aunty Jo sometimes promises not to do magic but then does it anyway. Luckily she is very good at magic. She has won lots of fairy prizes. Mummy hasn't won any fairy prizes, but I know she will one day.

As I ate my ice cream I was thinking hard. In science our teacher said that gravity makes things go down. But the colouring pens didn't go down – they went up in the air.

'How do science and magic both work?' I asked.

'You'll learn that at Fairy School,' said Mummy. 'When you're a big girl.'

'I still don't understand how they both work,' said Aunty Jo. 'But Mai does. You can ask her.'

★

When I got on the school coach to go to the science fair, my friends Tom and Lenka were already there. They had their model volcanoes too. Lenka's was really good. It had red crinkly paper and fairy lights.

My Not-Best Friend Zoe was on the coach as well, and her mother was giving out cookies.

'My mummy is the best,' Zoe was boasting. 'Look at her cookies. No one else has cookies.'

Aunty Jo looked at Zoe for a moment, then said, 'Wait a minute, Ella, I've forgotten something.'

She stepped off the coach, and a minute later she came back holding a plate of cookies. They were enormous, with sweets all over them.

'You're not the only one with cookies,' she said to Zoe with a nice smile. 'Ella has cookies too.'

'Look at those!' said Tom. 'They're epic!'

'They're awesome!' said Lenka.

Everyone wanted one of Aunty

Jo's cookies. No one was eating Zoe's mummy's cookies.

'Aunty Jo!' I whispered. 'Did you use magic?'

Aunty Jo just winked and passed me one. I knew Mummy would be cross if she found out, but I couldn't help feeling happy as I saw everyone eating the amazing cookies.

Zoe wasn't pleased, though. She looked at me with small angry eyes and I knew she would try to get back at me somehow.

★

The science fair was held in a great big hall. We put our projects on a special table. Then we walked around looking at all the displays. There were lots of tables where scientists were showing their experiments. One scientist had a model of all the planets.

Another one had some super-strong magnets that could make paperclips move without touching them.

'Cool!' said Tom as he watched. 'It's just like magic!'

I looked at Aunty Jo and she smiled at me. Then she said, 'Look, there's Mai!'

A woman was coming towards us. She had short dark hair and a sweatshirt

covered in numbers. She looked so much like a scientist that at first I couldn't believe she was a fairy too. But then I remembered that Mummy and Aunty Jo don't look like fairies either. And I don't look much like a Fairy-in-Waiting.

Mai was very friendly. She showed us her display. It had light beams that turned into rainbows. Then she asked, 'Are you interested in science, Ella?'

'Yes,' I said. I looked around to make sure no one could hear me, then I added, 'Science is like magic.'

'It's a different kind of magic,' said Mai, nodding. 'Being a Fairy Scientist is wonderful. It's the most exciting kind of scientist you can be. Maybe one day you will be a Fairy Scientist.'

I decided I would definitely be a Fairy Scientist when I grew up. And have a unicorn. Both.

'Let me come and see your project, Ella,' said Mai, and we walked over to the project table. She looked at all the model volcanoes, but we couldn't see my volcano anywhere. I started to feel worried. I knew I had put it on the table.

'Where's my volcano?' I said. 'I can't be in the competition if I don't have a volcano.'

'Don't worry!' said Mai. 'I'll ask the lady in charge if she's seen it.'

As she was walking away I noticed Zoe standing nearby, watching us. 'Have you lost your project, Ella?' she said in a mean voice. 'What a shame.' Then she laughed her horrible laugh and ran off.

I felt sure she had something to do with my disappearing volcano. I looked at Aunty Jo and I could tell she was thinking the same thing, because her face was all cross.

'I'll make you a new volcano,' she said. 'An even better volcano. I'll make sure you win the competition, Ella.'

'Aunty Jo!' I said quickly. 'Remember what Mummy said!'

But she wasn't listening. Aunty Jo marched off behind a screen and I guessed she was turning into a fairy. Suddenly I heard her say, **'Volcaneridoo!'**

She was doing magic!

A few moments later she came back, looking normal and holding a model volcano. I stared at it, astonished.

It was made out of painted cardboard, just like my volcano, but it was huge and had real flames bursting out of the top and it was making loud exploding noises.

Bang!

BOOM!

Sizzle!

'There!' said Aunty Jo, looking pleased. '*There's* a project for you.'

'Is that real fire?' I gasped.

'It's Fairy Fire. Don't worry – it can't burn you. Isn't it great?' said Aunty Jo, looking pleased with herself.

But a man walking past didn't think it looked great. When he spotted the volcano, he shouted, 'Fire! Fire!'

Then two children nearby started shouting, 'Fire!' and soon there was a crowd of people around us, all shouting, 'Fire! Help! Put it out!'

'It's *supposed* to be on fire!' said Aunty Jo, rolling her eyes. 'It's a volcano! Didn't you learn that in science, any of you?'

'Aunty Jo,' I begged, 'can't you put the fire out?'

'But then you won't win the prize,' she said. 'Ooh, look, it's going to explode again.'

The volcano made a massive exploding noise –

boom!

– and flames leaped up to the ceiling. Some of the children started crying and some were laughing and one boy shouted, 'Again! Again!'

'*Freezeridoo!*' came a loud voice behind us, and I turned round to see Mai. She had turned into a fairy, with huge shimmery wings and a glinty metal crown, and she was holding a Computawand.

All the people at the fair had frozen still like statues. No one could see or hear us.

'Jo!' said Mai Fairy crossly. 'What are

69

you doing? This is a science fair, not a Fairy Fair.'

'I know,' said Aunty Jo, biting her lip. 'I'm sorry. I just wanted Ella to have a great project. It's not fair. Ella worked very hard at her volcano and I *know* Zoe did something to it.'

Mai Fairy looked at me. And then she looked at Zoe, who was frozen nearby. Then she said, 'Let's see what happened to your volcano, shall we, Ella?'

She pressed an extra-long code on her Computawand – *bleep-bleep-bleepitty-bloop* – and said, 'Trackeridoo!'

At once a beam of light came out of her Computawand. We followed it to a table at the side of the hall. The light beam was shining brightly on a bin under the table – and in the bin was my volcano.

I grabbed it out of the bin at once and stroked it. 'My volcano!'

I was so happy to see it again. It was a bit bashed up but that didn't matter, because volcanoes are bashed up anyway.

'And let's see how it got there,' said Mai Fairy. She pressed another really long code – ***bleep–bleep–bleepitty–bloop*** – and another beam of light came out of her Computawand. This time it shone straight at Zoe.

'Oh dear,' said Mai Fairy, looking sad. 'Why would another girl want to put your volcano in the bin, Ella?'

'She was cross because Aunty Jo made magic cookies that were better than hers,' I told Mai Fairy.

Mai Fairy gasped. 'Jo! You used magic *twice* today? At a school?'

'I'm sorry!' said Aunty Jo again. 'Sorry, Ella.'

'But Zoe is always mean to me,' I told Mai Fairy. 'That's why she is my Not-Best Friend.'

Mai Fairy thought about this for a moment – then she smiled. 'I'll

tell you something, Ella,' she said.
'Sometimes people are mean to me.'

'No they're not,' I said, because grown-
ups aren't mean. Not mean like Zoe.

But Mai Fairy nodded. 'Yes they are.
They say mean things about my work.
And there are lots of things I could do. I
could do a magic spell on them and make
their noses turn green. Or I could cry. Or
I could give up.' She looked at me and
said, 'What do you think I do, Ella?'

I wanted to say, *You turn their
noses green*, but I knew that wasn't

the right answer. 'I don't know,' I said, and Mai Fairy smiled.

'I remember that I am a strong fairy. I say, "Sorry, I'm too busy to listen to you right now." And I just carry on with my work.' Mai Fairy patted my hand. 'Now, go and put your volcano on the table, while I use some Fairy Dust so none of the people here will remember what has happened,' she said.

I put my model volcano carefully on the table while Aunty Jo Fairy and Mai Fairy sprinkled Fairy Dust all over the people at the fair. For about ten seconds everyone was completely still. They had sort of gone to sleep. Then . . .

'Go!' said Mai, and they all woke up.

Then she said, 'Treacle tart!' and instantly she was normal again.

At once Zoe saw me by the display table, and she came running up.

She stared at my volcano as though she couldn't believe her eyes.

'You found your volcano!' she said. 'I don't understand. You *found* it.'

'Yes,' I said. 'I did. Wasn't that lucky?'

★

When they gave prizes out for the volcanoes, I didn't win one. Nor did Zoe. But Lenka did!

I gave her a big hug and said, 'Well done, Lenka!'

Then we were given sheets with pictures of volcanoes to colour in. I was colouring mine carefully when Zoe came up really close to me. She looked at me with her small angry eyes.

'I bet you feel stupid now, Ella,' she said. 'You made all that fuss about your volcano, but you didn't win.'

I looked at her for a moment. I thought about what Mai had said. I thought, *I am a strong Fairy-in-Waiting. And one day I will be a Fairy Scientist.*

Then I smiled at Zoe and said, 'Sorry, Zoe. I'm too busy to listen to you right now.' And I got on with my work.

POTTERIDOO!
Fairies behaving badly

It was Aunty Jo's birthday and we were wrapping her present. Mummy had bought her a new book called *Fairy Yoga*. We wrapped it up in flowery paper. I thought it looked lovely, but Mummy frowned.

'It doesn't look very special,' she said. 'Jo's presents always look special.'

I knew what she meant. On Mummy's birthday Aunty Jo had given her a present wrapped with six different kinds of ribbon and a flower decoration.

Mummy made a ribbon bow and tied it on to the present, but it didn't look very good. It was floppy and messy. Mummy pulled it around a bit, trying to make it look better, but all she did was rip the wrapping paper. She sighed and pulled the paper off the book.

'OK, that's it,' she said. 'I'm using magic.'

'Or we could just try again,' I said quickly – but Mummy didn't hear me. She stamped her feet three times, clapped her hands, wiggled her bottom and said, 'Marshmallow' . . . and **POOF!** she was a fairy. She pointed at the book, pressed a code on her Computawand – *bleep-bleep-bloop* – and said, 'Wrapperidoo!'

At once the book was covered in shiny silver paper, with gold ribbon and a huge gold pom-pom. It looked *amazing*.

'There!' said Mummy Fairy. 'Isn't that fantastic?'

Then, in front of my eyes, the TV was wrapped up. One minute it had been a normal TV. The next it was covered in shiny orange paper, with blue ribbon and a big bow.

'Mummy Fairy,' I said, 'look at the –'
Then I stopped and gasped, because now
the sofa was wrapped up too. It was
covered in red-and-white stripy paper,
with a tinsel bow. 'Mummy Fairy!' I said.
'Everything's being wrapped up!'

'Oops,' said Mummy Fairy, looking astonished. 'I don't know how *that* happened. Where did I put my Computawand?'

While Mummy Fairy looked around for her Computawand, the table was suddenly wrapped up in pink spotty paper, with three different-coloured ribbons. Then the lamp was covered in sparkly tissue paper and a velvet flower decoration.

I loved everything being wrapped up. It looked as if the room was filled with presents. In fact, it felt like Christmas!

'Here it is!' said Mummy Fairy as she found her Computawand under some wrapping paper. She quickly pressed a code – **bleep–bleep–bloop** – and said, 'Stoperidoo!'

We waited breathlessly for a little while, but nothing else got wrapped up.

Just then Daddy came into the room with Ollie. 'What on *earth* . . .?' he said, looking around.

'It will be a fun game for Ollie and Ella,' said Mummy Fairy firmly. 'They can unwrap all the furniture.'

Ollie loved it. He ripped all the paper off, shouting, 'Weezi-weezi-weezi!'

I tried to save the paper and keep it flat, so we could use it again.

'I'm just wondering,' said Daddy to Mummy Fairy. 'Is there a reason you wrapped up everything in the room?'

Mummy Fairy went a bit pink. She said, 'I wanted my present to look special. Jo's presents always look special.'

'Remember, life is not a competition,' said Daddy.

Then I remembered something I had once heard Mummy's Fairy Tutor Fenella say on FairyTube. I said, '*When fairies won't work together, magic goes wrong. When fairies work as a team, magic goes right.*'

'I know,' said Mummy Fairy. 'You're right. It doesn't matter whose present

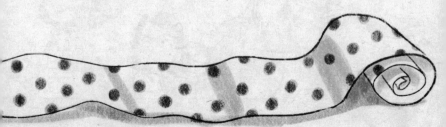

looks better.' But she stroked the big gold pom-pom on Aunty Jo's present and looked very pleased.

★

That afternoon Aunty Jo was having her birthday party at a special pottery shop. We could all go there and make something out of clay! I was very excited. Mummy and Daddy were there, and Aunty Jo and Granny. Ollie was there too, but he wasn't

allowed to have any clay because he would eat it, so he sat in a high chair.

We put on aprons and sat round a big table. The pottery teacher gave us lumps of clay and said we were each going to make a pot. 'You're all beginners,' she said. 'Your pots will be simple, but they can still be beautiful.'

She showed us how to make long sausages from clay and

wind them round and round to make a
pot. Then she said, 'I will be back in half
an hour,' and she went out.

The clay was all soft and squidgy and
I smooshed it with my fingers. It felt so
lovely. Then I started to roll out a sausage.
Daddy was rolling out his clay too.
Everyone was working very quietly.

Granny was finding it quite difficult.
She kept saying, 'This wretched clay won't
do what I want!'

Aunty Jo finished her pot first. It was
very nice, but a bit plain and a bit wonky.

She looked at it and frowned. 'Hmmm,' she said. 'I think this needs pepping up.'

At once Mummy looked up from her pot, which was also a bit wonky. 'Are you using magic?' she said. 'Are we allowed?'

'It's my party,' said Aunty Jo. 'Why shouldn't we use magic?'

'I agree,' said Granny, who had a smear of clay on her face and looked quite hot and bothered.

Mummy, Aunty Jo and Granny all got up from their seats. They stamped their feet three times, clapped their hands, wiggled their bottoms and said 'Marshmallow', 'Sherbet Lemon' and 'Extra-strong mint' . . . and **POOF!** they were fairies.

'Here we go!' said Aunty Jo Fairy, looking pleased. She pointed her Computawand at her pot and said, *'Potteridoo!'*

Straight away her pot turned into a wonderful vase.

'Very nice!' said Granny Fairy. She pointed her old-fashioned wand at her own pot and said,

'Potteridoo!' Her pot
grew big and round, with a
beautiful decorated edge.

'Very smart!' said
Mummy Fairy. She pointed
at her pot and said, 'Potteridoo!'
and hers turned into a lovely jug with
a handle.

'Ooh,' said Aunty Jo Fairy at once. 'I want handles.'

She pointed at her pot and said, **'Handleridoo!'** – and two handles appeared on her pot.

'I want handles too,' said Granny Fairy. **'Handleridoo!'**

'I want mine to be bigger,' said Mummy Fairy. **'Biggeridoo!'**

'I want *mine* to be the biggest!' said Aunty Jo Fairy at once. **'Biggesteridoo!** And I want a spout,' she added. **'Spouteridoo!'**

Mummy Fairy, Aunty Jo Fairy and Granny Fairy all started casting lots and lots of spells. They kept shouting **'Biggesteridoo!'** and **'Handleridoo!'** and waving their wands around while Daddy and I stared at them.

'It's not a competition,' said Daddy, but no one listened.

Soon all three pots had grown up to the ceiling. They all had lots of handles and strange wiggly bits. They were the silliest, ugliest pots I had ever seen. But

Mummy Fairy, Granny Fairy and Aunty Jo Fairy kept doing more spells on them.

Then Aunty Jo Fairy pointed at a piece of clay and said, 'Lideridoo!' But the clay didn't turn into a lid. It started whirling around the room. Then it started spattering itself over everyone.

'Help!' said Granny Fairy as clay hit her face. 'Naughty clay!'

'Weezi-weezi-weezi!' said Ollie, roaring with laughter and pointing at Granny Fairy.

Before long all the clay was flying around the room. The three pots were still growing handles and spouts. Mummy Fairy had clay in her ear and Aunty Jo Fairy had clay up her nose, but they were still waving their wands and casting spells.

'This is ridiculous!' shouted Daddy. 'It's not a competition! Tell them, Ella!'

'*When fairies won't work together, magic goes wrong!*' I called out. '*When fairies work as a team, magic goes right.* You have to use the Teameridoo spell!'

Mummy Fairy looked at me, panting, and said, 'What?'

'I learned about it on FairyTube,' I told her. 'When you need help to work as a team, you can use the Teameridoo spell.'

A piece of flying clay splatted into Mummy Fairy's face and she jumped. 'Ella, you're very clever,' she said. 'We have to work as a team or we'll *never*

get the clay back under control. Jo!' she shouted. 'Jo! Stop casting spells! We need Teameridoo!'

Aunty Jo Fairy looked cross. 'It's my birthday!' she said. 'I don't want to be in a team – I want to win!' But then a piece of clay whacked her on the head and she said, 'Oh, I suppose you're right.'

'Yes, dear,' said Granny Fairy, wiping clay off her glasses. 'This has gone too far. We have forgotten how to be good fairies.'

Mummy Fairy, Aunty Jo Fairy and Granny Fairy stood in a circle, ducking whenever the flying clay came too close. Mummy Fairy and Aunty Jo Fairy pressed codes on their Computawands and Granny Fairy waved her old-fashioned wand. Then they all said together, **'Teameridoo!'**

Just for a moment they all glowed, as though a light had shone on them. They

smiled at each other, and all the clay fell
to the floor. The room was calm again.
Everyone seemed happier.

'Phew!' said Daddy. Then we heard the
door open. 'Uh-oh. Our teacher is coming
back.'

Mummy Fairy looked at Aunty Jo
Fairy. Aunty Jo Fairy looked at Granny
Fairy. Then they all looked at each other.

'Toffee apple,' said Mummy Fairy.

'Blueberry pie,' said Aunty Jo Fairy.

'Flapjack,' said Granny Fairy.

Instantly they were back to normal

again. Then Mummy looked at the giant pots and gasped. 'We didn't change the pots back!'

'Too late,' said Daddy as the teacher came in.

'Hello!' she said. 'How did you get on?' Then she stared at Mummy in shock. 'Oh dear! You have clay all over you!'

'I was working very hard at my pot,' said Mummy quickly.

Then the teacher saw the three enormous pots. She turned quite pale and her eyes went very big. She looked

at all the handles and strange wiggly bits.
'Goodness,' she said at last. 'I've never seen
pots like these in my whole life.'

'Do you like mine?' said Aunty Jo.
'Mine is the one with six handles and
a spout.'

The teacher didn't seem able to answer. Then she saw Daddy's pot. 'Now this is a beautiful pot,' she said. 'It is plain and simple and has been carefully made. Well done!'

Daddy looked very pleased.

Aunty Jo made a sort of 'hmph' noise.

'This is also a very good effort,' said the teacher, picking up my pot. 'But you *all* did very well. It's not a competition,' she added.

'Quite right,' said Daddy, and I laughed. I was remembering the clay flying around the room. I wondered what

the teacher would have said if she had
seen that!

★

After we had finished at the pottery shop,
we went back to Aunty Jo's house for tea.
She opened her presents and we sang
'Happy Birthday' and ate delicious cake.
Then we watched Aunty Jo's favourite
film, *The Sound of Fairy Music*, while I
drew some pictures in my colouring book.
I drew all the strange pots, and giggled
because they looked so silly. I drew the
TV all wrapped up with a bow. Then

I thought about working in a team. I thought that when I was a big girl and went to Fairy School, I would always work together with other fairies.

'Mummy, how soon till I go to Fairy School?' I whispered.

'Not for a while yet, Ella,' Mummy whispered back.

'Because I can't wait to work in a fairy team.'

'You already do work in a fairy team, Ella,' said Mummy, holding my hand tight. 'And you're the best teammate ever.'

CATCHERIDOO!
Stop, thief!

We were going on a school trip to an art gallery and Mummy was coming too as one of the helpers. I was very excited!

As we set off for school that morning, Mummy was in a good mood.

'I've worked very hard this week, Ella,' she said, 'and today I want to have fun.'

It was a summer's day and Mummy was wearing a beautiful dress. We drove along and the sun shone through the car windows and I felt so happy. I couldn't wait to get to the gallery.

Miss Amy had told us all about art galleries at school. They were special places full of paintings and pictures. Some of them were by very famous artists. We would see pictures of people, pictures of different places, and pictures of animals. I wondered if I might see any pictures of fairies too.

Once we arrived at school, we got on a coach. There weren't any snacks because Miss Amy said we weren't allowed snacks this time.

It didn't take long to get there. The gallery was a big building with lots of windows and a massive escalator up to the top floor. When we saw it, my best friend Tom said, 'Wow!'

Then my other best friend Lenka said, 'I've never seen such a big escalator! It looks like a metal mountain!'

We wanted to go up and down the escalator lots more times, but Miss Amy said we had to go and look at the art.

So we walked along to a special room, which was really big with lots of paintings on each wall. There was a lady at the entrance and, as we arrived, she said, 'Welcome to the *Midsummer Night's Dream* exhibition. Who would like to wear fairy wings and elf hats?'

Everyone shouted, 'Me, me!'

I looked at Mummy and we shared a secret smile, because the fairy wings were very small and not shiny at all. But then they weren't real. Pretend fairies are never as good as real fairies.

I put on some fairy wings and Lenka put on an elf hat. Tom put on fairy wings *and* an elf hat, and we all laughed. Miss Amy put on some big fairy wings and said, 'Ella, I have some fairy wings for your mummy. Where has she gone?'

I looked around for her. Where *had* she gone?

Then she suddenly came out from behind a door – and she was Mummy Fairy! Her wings were huge and shimmery and they moved as she walked.

'I brought my own fairy wings,' she said, smiling at Miss Amy.

'Goodness!' said Miss Amy, staring at Mummy Fairy. 'They're wonderful! And what a lovely crown!'

I couldn't believe Mummy was being a fairy in front of everyone!

'Don't worry, Ella,' she said quietly. 'No one will guess. They think it's a costume. This is fun, isn't it?'

We all sat on the floor and the art lady talked to us about how to look at paintings. She told us that we must all try

117

to notice things. She said we could notice different shapes and colours. We could notice what people were doing in pictures, and what the weather was like.

Then we were allowed to walk around and look at the paintings as long as we behaved well. There were other people in the gallery too, and the lady said we had to be polite and not barge into them.

Some of the paintings did have fairies in them, just like I'd hoped. Mummy Fairy and I looked at a painting of a fairy sitting on a chair with a crown on her head. The painting was called *The Fairy Queen*.

'What do you notice, Ella?' asked Mummy Fairy.

'I notice that the fairy is beautiful,' I said. 'But she looks a bit cross.'

'I agree,' said Mummy Fairy. Then she added quietly, 'There's no one nearby. Shall we see what she'd look like with a smile?'

Mummy Fairy got out her phone and it turned into a Computawand. She quickly pressed a code – **bleep-bleep-bloop** – pointed it at the painting and said, **'Smileridoo!'**

Suddenly the fairy in the painting was smiling, and I couldn't help giggling. She looked *much* better with a smile.

Then Mummy Fairy pressed another code and said, '*Normeridoo!*'

The fairy was back to normal.

Then we walked on and looked at a painting with a gloomy sky.

'Let's improve the weather,' said Mummy Fairy.

She pressed the code, then pointed her Computawand at the painting. '*Blueridoo!*' she said. But instead of just the sky turning blue, the whole painting turned blue.

I gasped. 'Mummy Fairy! There isn't a

picture any more! There's just blue!'

'Oops!' said Mummy Fairy. 'I don't know how *that* happened.' She quickly pressed another code and said, **'Normeridoo!'** and the painting went back to normal. 'Maybe I'll leave the other paintings alone,' she said, and I agreed with her.

She put her Computawand away, just as Tom and Lenka came over.

'We've got to choose a picture and draw it,' said Tom. 'I'm drawing the one of the spooky forest. Which one will you draw, Ella?'

We walked around together and looked at all the pictures, and then I saw a painting of a mermaid.

'I'm going to draw the mermaid,' I said, and smiled at Mummy Fairy because we had once met real mermaids.

'Me too!' said Lenka. 'I love mermaids!'

The art lady gave us pencils and pieces of paper on boards. Lenka and I sat in front of the mermaid painting and tried to copy it. I noticed that the sea was wavy and the mermaid's tail was scaly. All of a sudden, just as I was trying to copy the pattern of the scales, I heard a man yelling.

'There's been a robbery!' he was shouting. 'Someone has

stolen a painting. *The Fairy Queen* has gone!'

We all gasped.

'A robber!' said Lenka. 'Let's catch him!'

The next minute, a bell started ringing. It was very loud, like a fire alarm.

'What a dreadful thing to happen,' said Mummy Fairy, looking serious.

'Don't worry!' called out Miss Amy. 'Everyone, stay still!'

But no one
stayed still. We
had all got up to
try to catch the
robber. Lenka and I
were looking all around.
Tom was practising his
kung fu moves.

'When we find the robber, I'll do kung
fu on him,' he said in a fierce voice.

Tom is really good at kung fu. I
thought the robber should watch out.

Suddenly we all saw a man in a black

coat running to the door.

'There!' shouted Lenka. 'There he is!'

She started running towards the man, but two guards in uniform had already grabbed him.

'Where is the painting?' asked one of the guards, sounding very stern. 'Do you have it?'

'No!' said the man. 'I'm not the robber! I was running because I was scared of the robber!'

He took off his coat and emptied his pockets but there wasn't a painting anywhere.

'Are you hiding it in your hat?' said the other guard.

'I haven't got a hat!' said the man. 'I tell you, I'm not the robber!'

I looked around the gallery and noticed a woman in a pale coat. She was holding her coat very carefully, as though she was hiding something, and creeping towards the door.

'Mummy Fairy!' I whispered. '*That's* the robber!'

Mummy Fairy looked at the woman and her eyes widened. 'I think you're right, Ella,' she whispered back. 'We need to catch her!'

Mummy Fairy got out her phone and it turned into a Computawand again. She pressed a code – **bleep-bleep-bloop** –

pointed it towards the woman and said,

'Catcheridoo!'

But, as she said this, the woman hurried

quietly across the room and out of the

gallery. No one else had seen her, because

everyone was looking at the man and the

two guards.

'I missed her!' said Mummy Fairy,

looking cross. 'She was too quick for me!

Come on, Ella – let's get her!'

We ran after the woman, but she was

really fast. As we burst out of the door we could see her. She was already on the escalator down and she was nearly at the ground floor. No one else was around to stop her.

'We'll never catch her!' I said. 'She'll escape!'

'No she won't!' said Mummy Fairy. She pointed her Computawand at the escalator, quickly pressed a code – *bleep-bleep-bloop* – and shouted, 'Reverseridoo!'

At once the escalator changed direction. Instead of being a down escalator, it was an up escalator. It started bringing the woman towards us!

The woman looked so shocked that I started giggling.

'Stop it!' she said angrily. 'I need to go down!'

'You're coming up,' said Mummy Fairy. 'And you're giving back that painting.'

The woman started trying to run down the escalator, even though it was going upwards.

'No, you don't!' said Mummy Fairy. She pressed another code – *bleep-bleep-bloop* – and said, **'Speederidoo!'**

The escalator sped up. It whizzed the

woman all the way back up to the top.
She stumbled off and her coat fell open –
and there was the painting of the Fairy
Queen!

Mummy Fairy grabbed the woman's
wrist and yelled, 'We've found the
painting! Come
quickly! Guards!'

The woman was wriggling, trying to escape, but she couldn't.

She glared angrily at Mummy Fairy. 'You're very strong,' she said. 'Do you have special powers or something?'

'I go to the gym,' said Mummy Fairy, smiling.

The two guards came running over and one grabbed the painting. 'This is it!' he exclaimed. 'You've caught the robber! Well done!'

The other guard was looking at the escalator in surprise.

'The escalator's broken!' he said. 'It's going the wrong way. And it's too fast. We'll have to fix that.'

'Yes,' said Mummy Fairy, winking at me. 'You will. I have no idea how *that* happened.'

★

We didn't look at any more paintings after that. The gallery was closed for the rest of the day, so we went to the cafe for lunch. Mummy Fairy turned back into a normal mummy and told Miss Amy that she had taken off her wings.

While we were all sitting at a big long table eating our lunch, the art lady came to talk to us.

'I want to say a big thank you to Ella and her mother for finding our painting,' she said. 'We are very grateful to you. Well done!'

Everyone clapped, and Tom shouted, 'Hip hip hooray!'

'It was Ella who was the detective,' said Mummy. 'She saw the woman creeping away.'

'It just shows,' said the art lady, 'how

important it is for us to use our eyes and notice things. Ella, you noticed more than anyone else in this gallery today.'

As a reward she gave Mummy and me a present each. It was a voucher for the gift shop. We could both choose a poster of one of the paintings from the gallery. I was very excited. I would put the poster up in my room and look at it every day.

'Which poster will you get?' Lenka asked us. 'Will you choose the Fairy Queen painting?'

'Yes, I think will,' said Mummy. 'It'll remind us of our adventure. Even if she does look a little gloomy. And I think I can guess which painting Ella will choose . . .'

'The mermaid!' I said immediately, and Mummy said, 'I knew it!'

And we both smiled.

TEST YOUR

Fairy Skills

Turn the page for lots of fun activities!

You can find all these activities at
www.puffin.co.uk/mummyfairy,
where you can print them out and test
your fairy skills again and again!

MERMAIDERIDOO!

Draw yourself as a magical mermaid –
remember to colour it in!

FINDERIDOO!

Can you spot these sea creatures
in the word search?

(Remember to look horizontally, vertically and diagonally.
Answers on page 150.)

CRAB   SEAHORSE

FISH   SHARK

MERMAID   STARFISH

OCTOPUS   WHALE

D	K	A	H	F	W	E	A	S	V	I	D
X	O	S	P	S	E	A	H	O	R	S	E
P	I	H	N	O	V	G	F	Q	O	H	P
F	L	C	D	V	A	T	U	I	R	A	Y
J	S	A	R	H	L	P	Q	N	T	R	E
Q	U	O	B	A	S	E	P	D	X	K	O
W	P	J	W	Z	B	I	I	Y	E	A	M
A	O	B	H	U	V	A	F	K	Y	E	G
Y	T	N	A	K	M	E	I	R	F	B	H
R	C	S	L	R	C	U	L	G	A	R	E
I	O	A	E	H	B	I	R	M	O	T	L
Z	C	M	C	T	D	S	O	T	E	K	S

COLLECTERIDOO!

Some litter has suddenly washed
up on the beach!

Can you spot the eight differences

between the two pictures?

(Answers on page 150.)

VOLCANERIDOO!

How to make your very own erupting volcano
and become a fairy scientist!

WHAT YOU NEED:

★ 1 small empty plastic bottle
(with the cap removed)

★ Brown or black modelling clay

★ Eco-friendly glitter (optional)

★ A tray (optional)

★ Funnel

★ Bicarbonate of soda

★ Food colouring

★ Vinegar

WHAT TO DO:

1. With a grown-up's help, use modelling clay to cover a small plastic bottle until the clay forms the shape of a mountain.

2. Leave the clay to dry until it is nice and hard. You can add some glittery sparkle now if you want to transform it into a fairy volcano!

3. Now for the magical part! You'll need to take your volcano outside or put it on a tray – just in case you haven't got a Computawand to help you clean up.

4. Using the funnel, put three tablespoons of bicarbonate of soda into the bottle.

5. Add a few drops of food colouring. Volcanos usually erupt with red lava, but magical lava can be any colour!

6. Finally, pour in a cup of vinegar and say, **'Volcaneridoo!'**

7. Wait for the volcano to magically erupt. Once it has fizzed out, you can wash your volcano and do your spell again and again!

ANSWERS

FINDERIDOO!

COLLECTERIDOO!

150

Have you read all of Ella's adventures with Mummy Fairy?

Also available as audiobooks!

ABOUT SOPHIE KINSELLA

Sophie Kinsella is a bestselling author and the adventures of Ella and Mummy Fairy are her first stories for children. Her books for grown-ups have sold over forty million copies worldwide and have been translated into more than forty languages. They include the Shopaholic series and other titles such as *Can You Keep a Secret?*, *The Undomestic Goddess*, *My Not So Perfect Life*, *Surprise Me*, *I Owe You One*, and *Finding Audrey* for young adults.

You can find out more about
Sophie's books on her website:
www.sophiekinsella.co.uk